TOOT

Goes to Dinosaurland

For Ruben

First published in 2014 by Nosy Crow Ltd
The Crow's Nest, 10a Lant Street
London SE1 1QR
www.nosycrow.com

ISBN 978 0 85763 240 1 (HB)
ISBN 978 0 85763 241 8 (PB)

A CIP catalogue record for this book is available
from the British Library.

Printed in China

1 3 5 7 9 8 6 4 2 (HB)
1 3 5 7 9 8 6 4 2 (PB)

Catherine and Laurence Anholt

TOOT

Goes to Dinosaurland

nosy crow

TOOT the bunny hops out of bed.
"Good morning, little car," he says.
"Toot, toot!" says the little car.

TOOT loves his little car.

He gets a hanky and polishes
the lights . . . rub, rub, rub!

TOOT climbs inside and
beeps the little horn . . .
toot, toot, toot!

Then TOOT turns the key
and starts the little engine . . .

bro-o-om,
bro-o-om,
bro-o-om!

"Hmm!" says TOOT.
"I'll push the purple button.
Let's go to . . .

Dinosaurland!"

Into a tunnel . . . lights on!

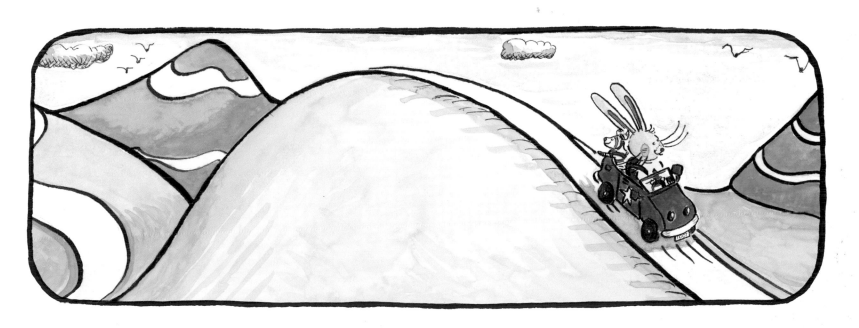

Up and down the mountains . . . whee-hoo!
Look out, here we come!

The little car comes to the top
of a high hill.

"Look!" says TOOT.
"Dinosaurland!"

TOOT meets a weeny dinosaur –
"Hello, weeny dinosaur," says TOOT.

TOOT meets a middle-sized dinosaur –
"Hello, middle-sized dinosaur," says TOOT.

TOOT meets a big dinosaur –
"Hello, big dinosaur," says TOOT.

"I'm glad there wasn't a **huge enormous dinosaur,**" says TOOT.

The little car flashes its lights and waves its wipers.

"I'll push the green button," says TOOT.

"Let's go . . .

HOME."

Go, TOOT, go!

Over the mountains . . . whee-hoo!

Through the tunnel . . .
lights on!

Over the city . . .
toot, toot, toot!
All the way home.

Then TOOT turns off
the engine . . .
bro-o-om, bro-o-om, shhh!

TOOT climbs
out of the little seat,
"Home again."

TOOT gets a hanky
and polishes the lights
. . . rub, rub, rub!

"Goodnight, little car," says TOOT.
"I wonder where we'll go tomorrow?"
"Toot, toot!" says the little car.